MONSTER RESCUE

OPERATION FIND CLEO!

MONSTER HIGH™

MONSTER
RESCUE

OPERATION FIND CLEO!

MONSTER HIGH™

MONSTER RESCUE
OPERATION FIND CLEO!

BY MISTY VON SPOOKS

(L)(B)

LITTLE, BROWN AND COMPANY
New York Boston

Little, Brown and Company

Hachette Book Group
1290 Avenue of the Americas, New York, NY 10104

Visit us at lb-kids.com

Little, Brown and Company is a division of Hachette Book Group, Inc. The Little, Brown name and logo are trademarks of Hachette Book Group, Inc.

The publisher is not responsible for websites (or their content) that are not owned by the publisher.

First Edition: December 2016

Library of Congress Control Number: 2016946561

ISBN 978-0-316-31569-2

10 9 8 7 6 5 4 3 2 1

LSC-C
Printed in the United States of America

CHAPTER 1

With her headphones on and the door shut tight, Draculaura sang her heart out as she danced alone in the moonlight. And why shouldn't she? No one could hear her. No one could see her. Usually, that bothered Draculaura—a lot. As a vampire hiding out in the Normie World, her entire life revolved around secrecy, sneaking, and skulking around to make sure that no human knew she even existed. Her dad, Dracula, insisted on it. After the great monster Fright Flight, monsters like Draculaura and her dad had gone into hiding for their own protection—leading to totally dull and lonely lives.

But even Draculaura had to admit that hiding could come in handy, like when she wanted to belt out the latest song by Tash, her all-time favorite musician, and practice some fangtastic new dance moves. Even so, she would have gladly given up complete and total privacy to have some ghoulfriends of her very own.

Draculaura was so caught up in dancing that she didn't hear the soft *tap-tap-tap* at her window. The tapping grew louder and she still didn't notice. Luckily, her pet, a spider named Webby, was paying attention. Webby swung in front of Draculaura and frantically pointed at the window to get her attention. Draculaura spun around to discover her dad hanging upside down outside, looking in.

"Come on, Draculaura," Dracula said. "Are you ready?"

Draculaura's eyes grew wider than the full

moon gleaming outside. "Oh! Right! It's tonight!" she exclaimed as she pulled off her headphones. Then Draculaura took a deep, steadying breath. "Right," she told herself. "I can do this!"

A worried frown flickered across Dracula's face. "But we don't *have* to do it right now," he said quickly. "Why don't we try it some other time? When you're more comfortable?"

Draculaura raised an eyebrow. "I'm comfortable now, Dad," she said. It was no surprise that he wanted to postpone her flying lesson. He would do *anything* to protect his only daughter.

"I'm just saying," Dracula said.

Draculaura rolled her eyes as she climbed out the window, but the truth was she thought it was totes adorable that her dad was as nervous about her first flight as she was. Maybe even more nervous! In her heart, though, Draculaura suspected that she and her dad were nervous for different reasons. Draculaura was jittery because she had no idea what it would be like to fly... but Dracula was worried because tonight would mark Draculaura's very first venture into the outside world.

The night sky sparkled with stars; the full moon hung so low that Draculaura thought she could reach out and grab it. In just moments, she would be flying through that velvety sky, free of the rambling old house high on Monster Hill. The house where Draculaura had grown up was enormous, with tons of turrets and perfectly creepy cupolas—but despite its massive size, it sometimes felt like more of a prison than a home. Draculaura's eyes were shining when she turned back to her father, but he didn't seem to share her excitement. He looked even more worried than he had before.

"Now remember, you can never be too cautious," Dracula told her. "The outside world is a scary place, filled with...*humans!*"

Draculaura pretended to cower as she covered

her face with her hands. "Oh no!" she said in a fake-scared voice. "Not the humans!"

"This is no laughing matter!" Dracula replied. "They may look innocent enough, but humans are one of the most dangerous species on earth."

But Draculaura was just getting started. "*Oooh, ooh*, dangerous? More dangerous than a swarm of killer robot bees? *Bzzzzzz!*" She darted and dodged around the rooftop pretending to be a bee in flight—but Dracula was not amused.

"I was about to make a very critical point," he said as he adjusted his heavy-rimmed glasses.

Draculaura had heard it all before—about a billion times. "Stay away from humans," she finished for him.

"*Stay. Away. From. Humans!*" Dracula repeated, emphasizing each and every syllable. "It's essential that you never let one see you. They're just not ready to accept us...at least, not yet. Promise me. Vamp's honor."

 5

"Ugh! I promise," Draculaura said, giving in. She knew there'd be no hope of free-flying if she didn't. "Now, if you don't mind..."

Draculaura squeezed her eyes shut, concentrating so hard that her whole face scrunched up. Then she took off running—first at a jog, then a sprint, then a sudden springing leap into the air, and—

Poof!

In one sudden motion, Draculaura transformed into a bat. There was just one problem: her wings.

Something was seriously wrong with them.

They were itty-bitty, like the wings of a baby bat. Totally useless for flying...or anything else. Draculaura fell down onto the roof with a *thud*.

"Ugh," she groaned as she morphed back into her vampire form. Dracula reached out a hand to help Draculaura pull herself up. Draculaura brushed the dust from her hot-pink skirt with the bat-shaped overskirt, a little embarrassed by her epic failure.

"Not all vampires get the bat transformation on their first try," Dracula said encouragingly. "Second time's the charm!"

Draculaura nodded, even more determined to succeed. She put all her focus and all her energy into psyching herself up, then took several steps backward until she was teetering on the very edge of the roof.

After taking a deep breath, Draculaura started to run, faster than she'd ever run before. Just before she reached the edge of the roof, she leaped, without even looking, and—

Poof!

"Yes!" Dracula cheered loudly as Draculaura transformed into a bat. "That's my ghou—*Ooh! Ow!*"

Dracula couldn't help cringing as he watched Draculaura's flying leap turn into a flying flop. She tumbled down to the ground, hitting every overgrown bramble bush on the way.

"I'm all right!" Draculaura cried.

Whomp.

"I got this!"

Whoomp.

"No need to help!"

Thunk!

With sticks and twigs poking out of her hair, Draculaura dragged herself back up to the roof. "Ugh. I can't do this. It's impossible!" she groaned.

"Not impossible—just challenging," Dracula told her. "Come on, let's try it together. One, two—"

Before he reached *three,* Dracula leaped off the roof and, with a wicked flip in midair, transformed into a bat! He flew around the rooftop, showing Draculaura how to do it by example.

Draculaura tilted her head, watching closely. She took a deep breath.

Here goes nothing, Draculaura thought.

She ran hard—

She leaped high—

Poof!

This time, it was different; Draculaura could feel it right away. Her wings were so *strong!* She flapped them with total joy as she soared into the night sky. "I did it!" she shrieked with glee. "Ha!"

"That's my ghoul!" Dracula said proudly.

Together, Draculaura and her father flew high over Monster Hill, their bat forms silhouetted against the golden moon. Draculaura's heart beat wildly; she almost felt dizzy, and it wasn't because of the high altitude. No, it was the feeling of freedom, of opportunity—the feeling that now that she was out of the house, *anything* could happen.

Anything was possible.

The human town glittered in the distance; even as Draculaura darted through the trees, doing her best to avoid the prickly branches, her gaze kept drifting over to the place where humans got to be this free every single day of their lives. *Do they have any idea how lucky they are?* she wondered wistfully.

Then something even brighter caught her eye. Just beyond the trees, an electronic billboard flashed with rapid pulses of light. Draculaura couldn't help it; she was drawn to it. A quick pivot, a fast flap, and she was on her way to take a better look—leaving her dad behind.

After a few moments, Draculaura realized that the billboard was playing a video of the one and only Tash! And that wasn't all. The billboard told Draculaura that Tash was about to launch a major tour for her new album—and she would be coming *here*!

Draculaura's eyes went all starry as she imagined it—Tash, coming to town, playing all of Draculaura's favorite songs, in person! It would be incredible—no, better than incredible, it would be—

Crash!

"Ow!" Draculaura cried as she spiraled down, down, down to the hard ground below.

Where had that telephone pole come from? Somehow, in the midst of her fantasy, Draculaura hadn't even seen it. She sat up and glanced around in embarrassment. Luckily, it didn't really hurt.

Who flies into a pole? she wondered, rubbing a small bump on her head.

With a sudden *whooosh*, Dracula landed by his daughter's side. "Drac! Drac, are you all right?" he exclaimed in concern.

"Yes, I'm fine—I think," Draculaura replied with a crooked smile.

"One must never get distracted while flying," Dracula replied. "Come on, let's get back up there."

Draculaura and her dad soared up into the night sky again.

"So...what were you thinking about, anyway?" Dracula asked.

Draculaura snuck another glance at the Tash

billboard, which seemed even more dazzling as they flew closer to it. *Would he understand?* she wondered.

There was only one way to find out.

"Pop, can I ask you something?" Draculaura asked in such a rush that her words came tumbling out. "Okay, there's this amazing girl, Tash, she's a big star and all the normal girls my age are obsessed with her—"

Draculaura could tell that, even in his bat form, her dad was frowning. "Normal girls?" he repeated. "You mean *human*—"

"Tash is totally, undeniably creeptastic!" Draculaura gushed.

"Cut to the chase," her dad replied.

"Can I go to her concert?" Draculaura begged. "It's only, like, three towns over, and I'll be super careful. *Pleeeease?* Pretty please with cobwebs on top?"

Dracula didn't even have to think about it.

"Drac, no, I'm sorry, it's just too dangerous," he replied firmly. "Monsters don't belong in the human world."

"But—please—" Draculaura began.

But Dracula didn't even let her finish. With a heavy sigh, he turned around and started flying back to their house on the Hill. The message was crystal clear: Their conversation was over.

If monsters don't belong in the human world, then where do I belong? Draculaura wondered.

She wasn't sure of the answer, but right now, Draculaura knew it wasn't the house on the Hill, not again, not tonight. She flapped her wings furiously—and sped off in the opposite direction.

"Drac! Wait!" Dracula called to her—but it was too late. Draculaura was already zipping through the night sky at a furious pace, darting and dodging streetlights and tree branches until she was sure she had slipped away. In a field of wildflowers just outside the human town, Draculaura landed.

She hid among the tall weeds until she spotted her father fluttering overhead, searching for her. Only then, after her father had flown past her, did Draculaura dare to transform into her vampire self. Her pale face was scrunched up in frustration.

"Argh!" Draculaura groaned. "Dad *always* says that—'the human world is too dangerous.' Well, *I'm* in danger of losing my mind!"

In the open clearing, Draculaura finally felt free enough to let out all her frustrations. At last, she could just be herself. After all, she was completely and totally alone—right?

"Drac!"

Dracula's voice echoed across the field to Draculaura. Even through she was annoyed, she couldn't miss the anxious edge to his voice.

"Draculaura, where are you?" Dracula called.

Draculaura knew what she had to do. With a heavy sigh, she transformed into a bat and flew up, up, up into the sky.

"I'm here, Dad," she said as she flew toward him.

A flicker of annoyance flashed through Dracula's eyes, but it was no match for the relief Draculaura saw there too. "What were you thinking?" he exclaimed. "Someone could've seen you!"

I highly doubt that, Draculaura thought—but she didn't say anything as she and Dracula flew back to the house on the Hill.

So much for her big adventure.

The moment the heavy door closed behind them, Dracula seemed to relax. "That wasn't so bad, was it?" he said. "We're home now, safe and sound."

"Yup," Draculaura said. "Safe and sound." Then she pretended to yawn. "I'm pretty tired from all that flying. I think I'll go lie down in my coffin."

Draculaura could tell she wasn't very convincing, but right now, she didn't really care. She had to escape to her room, away from her dad, who just couldn't understand how stifling their lonely lives were.

Back in her room, Draculaura flipped on her webcam and started pacing back and forth. "I mean, I'm almost sixteen hundred years old. I'm *extremely* responsible, I do *all* my chores, maintain every single cobweb in this house, and..." she ranted.

Draculaura leaned close to the webcam and lowered her voice before she continued.

"And I'll always be stuck here, hiding in the attic, hidden from the world," she continued glumly. But before she got too bummed, Draculaura managed a smile. "But at least I have you guys—my trusty *Vampology* vlog followers!"

With her fingers crossed, Draculaura snuck a glance at the computer screen. A small window listed how many subscribers she had: zero.

But surely somebody is out there—right? Draculaura wondered.

"Well, if any of my fellow weirdos are out there listening, have a good evening. I'm off to bed,"

Draculaura finished. Then, just as she turned off the webcam, she heard something behind her.

It was her dad—and from the look on his face, he had definitely overheard her. The only question was: How much did he know?

"Oh—er—I was just—uh—" Draculaura said nervously.

A strange half smile—part sympathetic, part concerned—crossed Dracula's face. "How about I make us a nice pot of bat tea?" he asked kindly.

Before Draculaura could respond, something completely unexpected—shocking, earth-shattering, even—happened.

The doorbell rang.

CHAPTER 2

Draculaura and her father stared at each other in horror. Well, Dracula was horrified. Draculaura didn't know how to describe how she was feeling—a thrill of excitement, a smattering of fear, and a whole lot of *whoa—what happens next?*

Neither of them spoke.

Then came another sound from outside: a heavy, insistent pounding.

Knock. Knock. Knock.

Draculaura raced down the stairs, with her

father following close behind her. He grabbed her shoulder and put his finger to his lips.

"Someone's at the door!" Draculaura whispered excitedly.

"Nobody's rung that bell for a hundred and fifty years!" Dracula hissed, running his fingers through his black-and-silver-streaked hair.

Then came another noise—one that was so unbelievable that, for half a second, Draculaura was sure she'd imagined it.

A voice.

"Hey! I know you're in there," someone said, her voice muffled by the heavy door.

She—whoever *she* was—knocked again.

"No one saw you—*right?*" Dracula asked.

"Of course not!" Draculaura exclaimed as loudly as she dared. But inside, she wasn't so sure. Had anyone seen her when she'd broken away from her dad and flown, wild and free, through the starry night? Or—even more risky—when she'd transformed, right there in the meadow, out in the open for anyone to see?

Nobody was around. I would've noticed, Draculaura thought—but suddenly, she couldn't remember if she'd even looked around to check.

The knock came again, louder this time.

"I saw you today!" the voice continued. "I saw you...turn into a bat!"

Draculaura's eyes went wide as her dad stared daggers at her.

"Oops," she said.

"You can open up," the voice continued. "I'm one of you!"

One of you.

Those three words—in that moment, they were *everything* to Draculaura. She rushed forward to peer through the peephole. Through the glass, she could see right away that the person on the doorstep was not a human. Not even close.

She was *definitely* a ghoul—and from the looks

of it, a cool one too. Her pale green face was all stitched up, and her mismatched eyes—one blue, one green—had monstrously long lashes. Even though she couldn't see through the peephole, the ghoul guessed that Draculaura was peeking through it. With a big grin, she unstitched her left hand and waved it in front of the door.

Draculaura gasped. This was it—the moment she'd been daydreaming about for ages! In one quick motion, she yanked open the door.

"No, what are you doing, she's—" Dracula began.

"One of us!" Draculaura squealed.

"Hi," the ghoul said as she stepped over the threshold, rocking a pair of lace-up platforms that showed off the delicate stitches connecting her feet to her legs. "I'm Frankie Stein."

Dracula opened and closed his mouth a couple of times, as if he wanted to say something but couldn't remember how.

Draculaura turned to him with a bright smile. "So..." she began, "how about that bat tea?"

A few minutes later, Dracula carried a tray with a teapot and three mugs into the drawing room, where Draculaura and Frankie were waiting for him. Draculaura was so excited she could barely sit still. But even though the plush velvet settee was perfect for bouncing, she forced herself to stay cool. She snuck a sideways glance at Dracula as he poured a cup of bat tea for Frankie. He hadn't said much since Frankie's unexpected entrance—and Draculaura had a funny feeling that his silence wouldn't last much longer.

"Thanks, Mr. D.," Frankie said as she took the cup of tea. "It's really lovely of you to have me stay here."

Dracula's forehead furrowed into a deep frown.

"She can share my bedroom!" Draculaura spoke up.

"Whoa, whoa, whoa," Dracula said, holding up his hands. "Let's just pump the proverbial brakes for a minute here."

Uh-oh, Draculaura thought. *Here it comes.*

"I haven't seen another monster in decades," Dracula continued. "We still don't know who she is—or where she came from, *hmm?*"

He didn't quite come out and say it, exactly, but Draculaura could read between the lines. Dracula was worried that Frankie was not who she seemed. That her very presence in their house spelled danger with a capital D.

Frankie, though, seemed totally unfazed. "Like I said, I'm Frankie," she told them. "My pops is Frankenstein. And after the great monster Fright Flight, he went into hiding like all other monsters. Things get a bit boring when you're hiding out all by yourself."

"Tell me about it!" Draculaura exclaimed. It was so fangtastic—she and Frankie had *just* met, and already they had so much in common!

Then Draculaura turned to her father. "Come on. You can't send her back. I never had a real friend before!" she pleaded.

"You have Webby!" Dracula countered.

"He's a spider, Dad," Draculaura replied. *"Pleeeeeeeease?"*

But Dracula shook his head. "My answer is final," he said firmly.

Draculaura made her eyes go all big and watery; her lower lip jutted out in a pout. It wasn't an act; she really did feel like she was about to cry.

"That's not going to work with me," Dracula said.

Frankie scooted over on the settee until she was right next to Draculaura. Her eyes were all big and watery too.

"I'm telling you, you're wasting your time,"

Dracula said. He looked at the floor, the ceiling, the shutters that were closed and barred on every window—everywhere *but* at the two ghouls. They both looked so sad and lonely and, well, *pitiful*...it was simply heartbreaking...

Dracula groaned as he buried his head in his hands. "Enough! Okay! She can stay!" he said, giving in at last.

Draculaura and Frankie jumped up, shrieking with glee, and shared a big hug. Then they both tackled Dracula with a hug—at the exact same time! He couldn't feel defeated for long—not when he saw how happy they were.

"Thank you, Dad!" Draculaura gushed. "This is the best—it's totally fangtastic—it's everything!"

Then Draculaura grabbed Frankie's hand. "Come on!" she cried. "I can't wait to show you my room...and we can hang out on the roof..."

"The roof?" Frankie asked excitedly. "Like... right out in the open?"

"Yes! I go up there all the time," Draculaura said. "You'll see, it's totally protected by the spires and turrets and stuff. You know what? We can have a sleepover up there! Let's go grab some stuff!"

A little while later, Draculaura and Frankie were sprawled out on the roof, staring up at a sky filled with twinkling stars. "Favorite color?" Draculaura asked.

"*Hmm* . . . electric blue," replied Frankie. "You?"

"Black. Definitely black," Draculaura said. "But also pink. Oh, oh, and sunlight!"

Frankie looked surprised. "You're a vampire— don't you burn in sunlight?" she asked.

"That's only in the movies," Draculaura assured her.

"Favorite song?" asked Frankie.

"That's a no-brainer," Draculaura replied right away. " 'Flawless.' It's Tash's new hit single."

"Who's Tash?" asked Frankie.

Draculaura sat bolt upright. "Who's *Tash*?" she

asked in astonishment. "Have you been hiding under a rock your whole life?"

"Not a rock—a secret lab, remember?" said Frankie.

Without another word, Draculaura dashed back into her bedroom and returned with her arms full of Tash swag: posters, fan magazines, T-shirts, CDs. She dumped the whole pile on Frankie's sleeping bag.

"Tash is the coolest, most awesome, amazing, beautiful rocker!" Draculaura gushed. "I have all her albums, and I've seen all her videos—even the really super-obscure one that she shot secretly in Tokyo—"

Frankie glanced down at Draculaura's massive Tash collection. She didn't seem impressed. "Oh. She's a Normie," Frankie said.

"What's that?" asked Draculaura, confused.

"Normie—normal," Frankie explained. "You know. A human."

Frankie's look—a mixture of skepticism and distaste—said it all.

Draculaura sighed. "Okay, big deal," she replied. "So she's a Normie. Don't you think it's a bit unfair that humans are the only ones who get to be 'normal'? I mean, who decided that turning into a bat and sleeping in a coffin was 'weird'?"

"Tell me about it!" Frankie exclaimed. "Just because I need a few stitches to stay together, that doesn't mean I'm not still a person!"

"Do you ever wonder what it would be like?" asked Draculaura. "To be...normal?"

Frankie shrugged. "I don't know," she said. "Being normal never really vibed with me. But it would be nice to do some 'normal' things. Like have friends."

"And throw parties!" added Draculaura. "And go outside during daylight."

"And hang out at a coffee shop and order elaborate-sounding drinks," Frankie said wistfully.

"It could be a coffin shop," Draculaura said.

"I love it!" Frankie exclaimed, clapping her hands. "And it could be right in the center of our little monster village, where monsters of all kinds could come to live together!"

"And go to school together," Draculaura whispered. The thought of a monster school—of friends—

It was enough to leave her breathless.

"A real school," Frankie echoed, pressing her greenish hand over her heart.

"We could call it…'Draculaura's Academy for Guys and Ghouls'!" Draculaura exclaimed. "And Beasties! And…Others!"

Frankie shot her a look.

"Yeah…no. Bad idea," Draculaura said quickly.

"What about…'School for the Scary, Strange, and Generally Unwelcome'?" suggested Frankie.

"Or we could just call it Monster High," Draculaura said.

The bolts on either side of Frankie's neck lit up like thousand-watt bulbs—but just as quickly, her smile faded. "If only we could." She sighed. "But it's impossible."

Draculaura tapped her fingers together, deep in thought. "Not impossible," she said. "Just... challenging."

She scrambled out of her sleeping bag, leaving it in a tangled heap on the roof. "Come on!" she said.

Frankie got up too. "Where are we going?" she asked.

"We can't have Monster High without students!" Draculaura announced.

A giant grin spread across Frankie's face as she understood what Draculaura meant. "Then let's go find us some monsters!" she replied.

The ghouls tiptoed silently through the house, careful not to disturb Dracula as they slipped out the door and into the wide world outside. Then, stifling their giggles, they took off running all the way to the human city, which Frankie called "Normie Town."

Their first stop was a deserted alley at the edge of Normie Town, a dank, shadowy place that seemed completely forgotten by the rest of the world. It seemed like the perfect spot for unwanted, unloved monsters to hide out—but Draculaura and Frankie didn't find anybody.

"What about over there?" Frankie asked, pointing to the moors. A damp mist rose from them; just the sight of it was enough to make Draculaura shiver.

"The moors?" she asked, frowning. "Nobody goes out there."

"Exactly!" Frankie declared. "It's the perfect hiding place for a monster!"

The fog grew thicker as the ghouls approached, but Frankie shot a bolt of electricity to light the way. Draculaura, however, slowed down.

"Maybe we should turn back," she said.

"*Umm*, hello? You're a vampire! You can't be afraid of the dark!" Frankie scoffed.

"Ha, ha!" Draculaura tried to cover up her jitters. "I'm not afraid of the dark; that's ridiculous— ha-ha-ha—*ahhhhhhhh!*"

Something burst from the shadows, tackling Draculaura and pinning her to the ground! Draculaura and Frankie screamed at the top of their lungs!

Suddenly, the wispy clouds parted; in the light of the full moon, Draculaura realized that she hadn't been attacked by some sort of menacing monster. It was a pack of squirmy, wriggly puppies!

The pups licked Draculaura's face, making her giggle. "Hey! Stop it! That tickles!" she cried.

"*Aww!* There's a whole pack of little pups," Frankie said as she reached out to pet one. "Aren't you just a wittle cutie-pie—"

Just then, a menacing growl cut Frankie's cooing short as a ferocious wolf bounded out of the shadows, its fierce fangs glinting in the moonlight. A terrible realization hit Draculaura and Frankie at the exact same time. They weren't surrounded by sweet little puppies.

They were surrounded by a pack of wolves!

Frankie helped Draculaura to her feet. Then the ghouls began to cautiously step backward.

"On the count of three, run," Draculaura whispered. "One—two—"

"Look at that—around the wolf's neck," Frankie interrupted.

Draculaura squinted her eyes and saw a bootiful moon-shaped amulet dangling around the wolf's neck.

"Kind of strange for a wild wolf to be wearing an amulet," Frankie continued. "Unless..."

"She's a monster!" gasped Draculaura.

The wolf snarled at the ghouls.

"I hope we're right," Frankie said nervously. Then she stepped forward. "Excuse me," she said in her most polite voice. "You wouldn't happen to be a...werewolf, would you?"

The wolf growled again.

"That's a shame," Draculaura spoke up. "'Cause we're looking for other monsters...like us."

The wolf stopped snarling. She tilted her head and stared at the ghouls with golden eyes.

"We're forming a high school up on the Hill— Monster High," Frankie said. "It's where monsters can go to be normal."

"Normal-*ish*," Draculaura corrected her.

"Right! And we're even gonna have a coffin shop," Frankie said, getting excited all over again. "With Mummy Mochas and everything!"

There was a sudden flash, so bright that even Frankie's electric bolts couldn't compare. Draculaura rubbed her eyes to clear her field of vision; when she looked up again, the wolf had vanished, replaced with a fierce ghoul with her hands on her hips and the most boo-tiful head of hair Draculaura had ever seen. The ghoul raised an eyebrow suspiciously at Draculaura and Frankie.

"I would howl at the moon for a Mummy Mocha," the ghoul said. "Are you ghouls for real?"

Draculaura sighed with relief as the puppies scampered around, transforming back and forth from wolf to human as they played.

"We're getting the monsters back together," Draculaura told the new ghoul. "You in?"

The ghoul looked ready to say yes—but something was holding her back. "I've got a lot of brothers," she began. "And my mom..."

"Well—we have some extra room in our house. I'm sure we—" Draculaura began.

But the ghoul didn't let her finish. "This... 'house,'" she said, like she'd never heard the word before. "Does it have more than one overly crowded bathroom?"

"Well…yeah," replied Draculaura.

At last, the new ghoul grinned. "Then I am *definitely* in," she replied. "I'm Clawdeen Wolf."

"Fangtastic!" Draculaura cheered. Their mission—Monster Rescue—was off to a clawesome start!

CHAPTER 3

The next night, Dracula tiptoed into Draculaura's room with two mugs of bat tea for Drac and Frankie. He noticed right away that her coffin bed was empty—then he spotted the three sleeping bags on the floor. But when Dracula pulled back the cover of one of the sleeping bags, he was so startled that he tossed the tea tray high into the air! Draculaura couldn't help giggling at the sudden bat-tea shower in her bedroom.

"Who is *this?*" Dracula demanded, pointing at Clawdeen. "Who is this *stranger?*"

Clawdeen bristled. "Who you callin' strange?" she snapped.

"*Daaaad!*" Draculaura groaned. "This is our *friend*, Clawdeen. She's a werewolf. We found her in the moors."

"And she really wants to live up here on the Hill," added Frankie.

Clawdeen nodded. "You got no idea what fifteen years of living in a den does to a ghoul's hair," she said, using her sharp claws to comb through her fangtastic mane.

"Can she stay, Dad?" begged Draculaura.

"No—and don't even try that sad-face routine," Dracula said. "That might have worked once, but I am not falling for that again."

It was too late, though. Draculaura was already looking up at him with wide, tear-filled eyes. Her pink lips jutted past her fangs in a pout; they started to tremble. And she wasn't the only one. Now Frankie and Clawdeen were staring up at Dracula with the same sad expression.

Dracula bit his lip as he tried, tried, *tried* to resist. "It's not even that cute," he said.

But it was effective.

"Okay!" he exclaimed, throwing his hands into the air. "But this is the last one!"

Ding-dong.

"Now who is *that?*" Dracula yelled as he hurried toward the door.

"Don't worry," Draculaura assured Clawdeen. "He's going to love the rest of your family, I just know it!"

Sure enough, the werewolf pups brought out Dracula's softer side—and before long, he was way more open to the idea of starting a school just for monsters. He just needed the chance to see how frighteous life could be with other monsters—instead of living in hiding.

As soon as Dracula was on board with Monster High, Draculaura and her ghoulfriends got to work turning the house on the Hill into a fangtastic high school. It already had a library filled with thousands of books about vampires, mummies, ghosts, werewolves, and monsters of all kinds. Next up, they renovated the cavernous dining room into a Creepeteria where hundreds of monsters could gather for meals. With Frankie's guidance, they turned the damp, dark basement into a high-tech lab for Mad Science classes. There was a math class for Clawculus and an entire wing devoted to Dead Languages. When the ghouls weren't spackling, plastering, or painting, they brainstormed all the different classes Monster High could offer. Haunting Music, Home Ick, Study Howl...Monster High was going to have it all!

There was just one more problem to tackle: the student body. *Whoever heard of a high school with only three students?* Draculaura thought, stifling a sigh as she glanced over at Frankie, who was poring over chemistry books, and Clawdeen, who was flipping through a fashion magazine. True, they were the best ghoulfriends she could imagine, but if Monster High was going to be everything she'd dreamed of, Draculaura knew that she had to find more students—stat.

She switched on her webcam and started another vlog post, telling any monster who might tune in just how much Monster High had to offer. "We're determined to rescue the monsters of the world," she said earnestly. "The freaky, the beastly, and the downright *weird*! Only—how do we find you?"

Draculaura refreshed the *Vampology* home page. Despite her hopes, the subscriber count was still a big, fat zero.

"Come on!" she groaned. "Isn't anybody listening?"

Frankie glanced up from her textbook. "You're

not gonna reach any monsters like *that*," she pointed out. "No wonder your vlog doesn't have any listeners. You're using the normal Internet!"

"Uh, yeah," Draculaura replied. "That's how it's done."

"*Uh, yeah,*" Clawdeen echoed Draculaura with a mischievous smile. "If you're *normal*."

"You gotta use the Monster Web," Frankie explained. She leaned over Draculaura and started typing on the keyboard.

"There's a Monster Web?" Draculaura gasped in surprise. She couldn't tear her eyes away from the monitor as the screen flickered, then transformed into a hot-pink-and-black background. With an expert click of the mouse, Frankie dragged Drac's vlog over to the Monster Web.

"Your TCP-IP-RIP ports are all glitchy," she told Draculaura. "You haven't even been broadcasting this whole time. But now, behold! The Monster Web! Available anytime, anywhere."

Frankie stretched and yawned, as if she hadn't just accomplished the most incredible thing Draculaura had ever seen.

"Mind. Blown," Draculaura breathed as she leaned closer to the monitor. Her hand was trembling with excitement as she refreshed the Web page.

And...nothing. Zero subscribers.

Disappointed, Draculaura turned around to ask Frankie and Clawdeen what else she could do. But the other ghouls were yawning as they crawled into their sleeping bags. Draculaura yawned too. It had been a long night. Maybe she'd come up with another idea tomorrow.

The next morning, Dracula was enjoying a hot cup of English Dreadfast tea when a sudden, piercing shriek shattered his peaceful breakfast. He leaped up from the table, sending his breakfast flying through the air, and raced through the house to Draculaura's room as fast as he could. By the time he flung open the door, Dracula was completely out of breath—but he still managed to ask, "What is it? Where is it?" in a total panic.

Then he paused, narrowed his eyes, and surveyed the scene. He couldn't see any threats. There was no sign of danger. And the three ghouls didn't seem scared or upset at all. Instead, they were clustered around Draculaura's computer, completely sucked into whatever was on the monitor.

Clawdeen glanced up and tossed her hair over her shoulder. "Er, where is what?" she asked.

"Whatever it is you were screaming about!" Dracula exclaimed.

When Draculaura looked up at her dad, her face was shining with excitement. "Monster High has students—*ahhhh!*" she shrieked gleefully. "I put out a call on my *Vampology* vlog—Frankie

44

taught me how to post it on the Monster Web—she's a tech *genius*! Anyway, we got, like, a zillion e-mails this morning!" Draculaura finished.

Clawdeen jumped up and down. "It's all happening!" she howled. "The monsters are coming! The monsters are coming! The—"

Clawdeen paused mid-jump as a new thought struck her. "Wait. How are they getting here?" she asked.

No one answered.

Suddenly, Frankie had a bright idea. "You can fly, right?" she asked Draculaura. She rubbed her hands together, creating a lightning bolt that jumped from one finger to the next. "Maybe if I just use my electricity to supercharge you…"

"Whoa, whoa, whoa, put it in reverse!" Dracula exclaimed, holding up his hands. "Nobody's electrocuting anybody here."

The ghouls exchanged a glance as Dracula rubbed his chin, deep in thought. He already knew they wouldn't give up, so he might as well make sure they did things in a way he approved of...

"If you're going to collect these monsters, you're going to do it the old-fashioned way," he finally said.

"I love the old-fashioned way!" Frankie said brightly.

"*And* you're going to wear helmets," added Dracula.

"Helmets?" Clawdeen repeated in disbelief. "You got any idea what a helmet will do to all this hair?"

Dracula gave her a pointed look. "Do you want to reach the other monsters or not?" he asked bluntly.

When he put it like that, even Clawdeen had to agree that helmets were a no-brainer. And that's how the three ghoulfriends found themselves decked out in the most fangtastic head protection that Dracula could scare up on short notice. That night, they all met up in the library.

 46

"Wait here," Dracula told them before he transformed into a bat. Then he fluttered up, up, up—all the way to the tallest rafters under the roof. Draculaura watched intently as her father pulled a dust-covered wooden box off the highest shelf. "Haven't used this thing in centuries," he called down to the ghouls. "Hope it still works."

"What exactly is it?" asked Frankie.

Dracula flew back to the group and carefully placed the box on the table before he transformed into his vampire form. "This is a Monster Mapalogue," he announced.

Then he removed the lid. The ghouls crowded around, eager to see what was inside as a warm pink glow shone from the box.

With great care, Dracula unlatched the sides of the box, revealing a wooden map covered with intricate carvings. Then he lifted up a glowing Skullette that dangled from a golden chain.

"Wow," Draculaura breathed.

"In ages past, monsters used the Mapalogue to locate one another. But when the humans turned against monsters during the great Fright Flight, our kind all went into hiding for our own protection," Dracula explained. "After that, there really didn't seem to be a use for this thing anymore."

"Until now!" Draculaura exclaimed as her dad reached forward and draped the chain around Draculaura's neck.

"So...how does it work?" Frankie asked.

"First, you place your fingers on the Skullette," Dracula explained. "Then you say the name of the monster you're trying to reach."

Draculaura checked her iCoffin. "First up is... Cleo de Nile," she announced. "The message is kind of choppy, but it sounds like she says that she's stuck—and ready to settle the score."

A worried expression flickered across Dracula's face. "Settle the score?" he repeated. "I don't like the sound of that. We're not about to—"

"Of course not, Dad," Draculaura interrupted him. "I'm sure that's just the way monsters feel after being totally alienated for hundreds of years. Once Cleo gets to Monster High, she'll be too busy to want revenge."

Dracula looked at Draculaura and her friends. "Are you *sure* you want to do this?" he asked the ghouls.

"Totes!" Draculaura said.

"Yes!" Frankie echoed.

"*Obviously!*" Clawdeen added.

Dracula took a deep breath to steady himself. "Okay," he said. "Say the magic words: *Exsto monstrum*. So all together..."

"*Cleo...Exsto...monstrum!*" Draculaura, Frankie, and Clawdeen chorused. Draculaura squeezed her eyes shut tight in anticipation...

But nothing happened.

Draculaura fought back a wave of disappointment. *We'll find another way*, she promised herself.

49

"Guess you were right, Mr. D.," Frankie spoke up. "This thing doesn't even—"

Whooosh!

In a flash, the ghouls vanished from the library—leaving Dracula all alone.

CHAPTER 4

An unseen force pulled Draculaura and her ghoulfriends through space, a lightning-fast trip that made everything blur in a flash of light and color. Draculaura held on tight—tight—*tighter* to the Skullette, wondering where in the world it would take them—

Pop!

The ghouls suddenly materialized in midair, where they hovered for a moment before falling down to the burning sand with a soft *thud*.

"Ow!"

"Ugh!"

"*Oof!*"

Draculaura sat up and looked around. As far as she could see in every direction was an endless expanse of grainy golden sand; the blazing sun overhead was blisteringly *hot*. Waves of heat shimmered as they rose from the ground. Against the brilliant, cloud-free sky, everything seemed to glitter. It almost made Draculaura woozy—or was that just her excitement at finding a new student for Monster High?

As the ghouls untangled themselves, Clawdeen knocked on her helmet appreciatively. "Guess these things come in handy after all," she said.

"The Mapalogue worked!" Frankie cheered. Then she glanced around. "But where's Cleo?"

"Ghouls! Over there!" Draculaura cried, pointing at a massive brick pyramid rising from the sand. "I think we've found our ghoul!"

 52

"You think Cleo's in there?" asked Clawdeen. "But there's a bunch of pyramids. Over there, and over there, and over there..."

Shielding her eyes from the bright sunshine, Draculaura glanced around. Clawdeen was right; there must have been several dozen pyramids dotting the desert.

"I trust the Monster Mapalogue," Draculaura said confidently, holding up the Skullette that still dangled around her neck. "I'm sure it brought us exactly where we need to be. And since that's the closest pyramid..."

"Then what are we waiting for?" asked Frankie. "Let's go!"

The ghouls hurried across the burning sand as quickly as they could. Inside the pyramid, it was surprisingly cool and as dark as a tomb. A series of small torches flickered unsteadily on the walls, but they were almost powerless to fight the all-encompassing darkness.

As her eyes adjusted to the dim light, Draculaura realized that hieroglyphs had been carved into the gold-plated walls. "Fangtastic!" she whispered as she brushed her fingers over them. "But... what are those?"

The ghouls examined two solid-gold sarcophagi in the very center of the tomb. One was big, the other was small; they were both covered in intricate hieroglyphs. "I wish I could read them," Draculaura said wistfully. "What do you think they say?"

"Probably 'Get out of my tomb unless you're cruising for a curse,'" joked Clawdeen.

"No way," Draculaura replied. "Cleo wouldn't curse us. She practically begged us to come rescue her."

"What makes you so certain that she's in a tomb?" Frankie asked practically. "Let's analyze what we know. Cleo is obviously wired in to current tech, right? Otherwise, how would she have checked out your vlog?"

"Yeah...and?" Draculaura replied.

"So if Cleo has all the latest tech, why would she be fanging out in some dark old tomb?" Frankie said. "It doesn't compute."

"But the Monster Mapalogue—" Draculaura began.

"Is, like, a billion years old," Frankie finished for her. "What if it malfunctioned or something?"

"Ghouls," Clawdeen interrupted them. "Who cares? Let's just open these tombs and get it over with. If we're not in the right place, we have other pyramids to check out."

As Clawdeen reached forward, Draculaura stopped her. "Wait, wait, wait!" she exclaimed. "Which one are you going to open?"

Clawdeen shrugged. "Both, if I have to," she replied. "Here we go!"

A metallic *scraaaaaaape* echoed off the tomb walls as Clawdeen pushed the lid off the smaller sarcophagus. Draculaura held her breath as suspense mounted; the sarcophagus almost looked too small to hold a person. *Monsters come in all shapes and sizes*, Draculaura reminded herself. In just another moment, the lid would be open, and all would be revealed—

"*Meow!*"

Draculaura's mouth dropped open as a mummified cat jumped out of the small sarcophagus!

"*Awww!*" Clawdeen cooed as the mummy-cat wrapped itself around her ankles, purring so loudly that the ghouls could hear it even through the bandages. "Not quite the monster I expected, but he's adorable!"

Draculaura knelt down to pet the cat. The yellowed bandages had been expertly wrapped around the cat; only one or two had started to unravel, even though they were clearly thousands of years old. Two slits had been cut for the cat's emerald-green eyes, which were the same color as the bejeweled tag that hung from its collar.

Draculaura leaned over to take a closer look. "Anubis," she read. "That's your name, huh? I like it. We can call you Nu for short."

"Cats are highly intelligent, you know," Frankie spoke up. "It's no accident that the ancient Egyptians worshipped them."

"You really wanted out of that sarcophagus, didn't you?" Draculaura asked Nu as she scratched behind his ears. "Who can blame you? I know what it's like to be locked up all by yourself for hundreds of years."

Then Draculaura turned back to Clawdeen and Frankie. "Poor Cleo. We've got to get her out of here!"

Draculaura strode over to the larger sarcophagus and used all her strength to pry open the heavy gold lid. "Hang—on—Cleo—" Draculaura said, grimacing as she pushed at the lid. "We'll—get—you—out."

With a deafening *boom*, the lid clattered to the

floor, sending a shock wave through the pyramid that knocked Draculaura, Frankie, and Clawdeen down. A thick cloud of choking black smoke surrounded them, making it impossible to see what was happening.

Coughing, Draculaura tried to wave the smoke away with her hand. A strange noise rumbled through the pyramid—it sounded like thunder, but more intense, more *menacing*—

"Wh-what's that?" she whispered to her ghoulfriends.

"I think…Cleo's growling at us," Frankie replied.

"Um…I'm not sure that's Cleo," Draculaura said.

Something inside the sarcophagus stirred.

"Do you think it's a curse?" whispered Clawdeen.

"No." Draculaura gulped. "I think it's even worse!"

Nu backed into a corner, hissing and spitting

through his bandages—which only confirmed Draculaura's fears.

The sarcophagus trembled as someone—or *something*—inside it moved. The ghouls watched in horror as an enormous mummy, more than eight feet tall, pulled himself up. Through the bandages, they could see his red eyes, glinting with rage. It was clear that he did *not* want to be awakened.

"My…eternal…slumber…" the mummy bellowed in a hollow voice.

"I can't say I blame him," Clawdeen murmured. "I'm an absolute beast without my beauty rest."

At the sound of Clawdeen's voice, the mummy's head whipped around. He took a shambling step toward them.

"Sorry we woke you," Draculaura said nervously. "Uh—we'll just be going now. Bye!"

But that wasn't good enough for the mummy. With a pyramid-shaking roar, he overturned the heavy gold sarcophagus as if he were kicking a tin can down the street.

He lunged at the ghouls, moving so fast that Draculaura and her ghoulfriends had to scramble to get out of the way.

"What are we gonna do now?" Frankie gasped.

Only one word came to Draculaura's mind.

"Run!" she screamed.

CHAPTER 5

Draculaura grabbed Clawdeen's and Frankie's hands and dragged the ghouls into a narrow tunnel that jutted off the side of the chamber. "If we can just get out of here," she said between gasps, "Mr. Mummy can go back to sleep, and we can all pretend that this whole thing never happened."

"But which way is *out?*" Frankie asked, panting as they ran.

"Um…I'm not sure," Draculaura admitted. "But

I'm sure this tunnel has to lead somewhere...
maybe there's an emergency exit or something..."

"I sure hope so," Clawdeen shrieked. "Because
this is definitely an emergency. Don't look now,
but the mummy is *following* us!"

Glancing backward was the *last* thing Draculaura wanted to do, but she couldn't help herself;
she peeked behind just in time to see the mummy
lift his bandaged hand and point it at her. A low,
mumbling noise echoed down the corridor—

"Ghouls!" she shrieked. "I think he's *cursing* us!"

Zing!

A blast of greenish light zipped past Draculaura, just inches from her face; it hit the tunnel
wall in front of them and left a smoking crater in
its wake.

"Are you kidding?" she yelled.

"That's my ghoul, you nasty used-up bandage!"
Clawdeen cried. "You better watch your—"

Zing!

 62

Another curse, another narrow miss. This one, however, exploded into thousands of small snakes, which started slithering in all directions.

"If I'm not mistaken, those are juvenile asps," Frankie yelled.

"That's all you got? Baby snakes?" Clawdeen hollered at the mummy.

"Some baby reptiles are even more poisonous than the adults," Frankie told her.

Clawdeen blanched. "In that case…let's get out of here, ghouls!"

Zing! Another curse exploded, raining dagger-sharp shards through the tunnel. It was clear to all the ghouls that the mummy was definitely upping his game.

"Look—the tunnel splits into a fork up ahead," Draculaura gasped. "I have a plan. If we split up, I think we can lose him—"

"He's still gonna chase one of us, Draculaura," Frankie pointed out. "It's not safe."

 63

"*This* isn't safe!" Draculaura countered as another curse exploded near their feet. "Just trust me on this, okay? I'll distract him, and you two—*run!*"

"Wait—" Clawdeen began.

But it was too late. Draculaura was already running, running—she leaped into the air with all her might and—

Poof!

Just like that, Draculaura transformed into her bat form. She flapped her wings as hard as she could—she wobbled once, twice, and then found her way.

Draculaura glanced down to see Clawdeen and Frankie standing there, totally awestruck. "I mean it, ghouls!" Draculaura called. "*Run!*"

Then, mustering all her courage, Draculaura flew right at the mummy!

At first, the mummy didn't notice the small bat winging her way toward him. Draculaura got close enough to claw at his bandages. Then she propelled herself into the air just as he tried to grab her.

"Too slow!" Draculaura yelled. "Is that *really* the best you can do?"

The mummy roared with rage as Draculaura dive-bombed him again. She snuck a quick glance at her ghoulfriends, who were nearing the end of the corridor. *Go, go, go,* Draculaura thought. She had to make sure her ghoulfriends made it to safety.

She dashed down and flapped her wings right in the mummy's face!

The mummy threw his head back and howled. He flung a fast succession of curses wildly into the air—*zing! zing! zing!*—but all they did was hit the tunnel walls.

Flying near the ceiling of the tunnel, Draculaura was covered in a sudden shower of dust, making her cough and sneeze. At first, she thought the mummy had finally landed a direct hit.

Then she realized that his wildly flung curses were taking a toll. Not on Draculaura or her ghoulfriends, but on the ancient bricks that had been used to build the pyramid. There was a crack snaking across the ceiling...if the mummy wasn't more careful with his curses, he would bring down the whole pyramid!

I've gotta get out of here, Draculaura realized. *But what about Frankie and Clawdeen? Where are they?*

Draculaura glanced around wildly—just in time to see her ghouls disappear down the fork in the tunnel. *Yes!* she cheered to herself. She'd launch one more attack against the mummy—hopefully that would buy enough time for her ghouls to get out of this pyramid before they were cursed or, even worse, buried alive!

Draculaura took a deep breath. The mummy's glowing eyes were the brightest thing in the tunnel. She could see him approaching, one shambling step at a time—

Flap-flap-flap-flap-flap.

Draculaura flew furiously toward the mummy, getting as close as she dared, and flapped her wings right in his bandaged face. *Whoosh!* A cloud of brick dust flew off her wings—right into the mummy's eyes! The gritty dust was fine enough to get through the linen bandages, making the mummy cough and sputter as he clawed at his face.

Now's my chance, Draculaura thought as she flew over the mummy, back down the dark and dingy tunnel. She could see a light gleaming up ahead—it had to be the main burial chamber, with all those burning torches. What a welcome sight they'd be after the bleak blackness of the tunnel!

Almost there, Draculaura thought.

And then she heard—

No, it couldn't be—

But it was. A single backward glance told her that the mummy was still chasing her!

Draculaura burst out of the tunnel, back into the gold-walled burial chamber, past the two sarcophagi, which were both still empty.

The mummy was just steps behind her.

Draculaura reached way down deep for one more burst of energy, then flew even higher. She was using every ounce of her strength—but would it be enough? She was so new at flying... and her wings were tired and felt as heavy as lead. Despite her height, the mummy was gaining on her—she didn't dare turn around to look, but she was sure she could feel him approaching as he got even closer...she could just picture his arms reaching out, trailing those grubby old bandages...

Faster! Draculaura thought frantically. One last burst of speed and strength and she was *out!* Out in the open, against that wide blue sky, under that blistering gold sun! Forget black and hot pink—in this moment, sunlight was *definitely* Draculaura's favorite color.

Pop!

Draculaura transformed back into her vampire self and fell onto the sand, giving her tired arms a much-needed break. She closed her eyes in relief and basked in the sunshine.

"Arrrrggggghhhhh!"

Draculaura's eyes popped open. It was the mummy—and he was still careening toward her!

"Give it a rest, Bandage Breath!" Draculaura hollered as she scrambled to her feet. But beneath the tough talk, she was worried—*really* worried. What if the mummy charged out of the pyramid and followed her onto the sand? She was totally worn out from her wild flight...but he had obviously been resting for the last millennia or two, and clearly he had plenty of energy to burn.

Draculaura ducked behind a gleaming statue

of a winged lion, but she knew the hiding place wouldn't keep her safe if the mummy left the pyramid. She didn't have a choice: If he came after her, she'd have to run.

What else could she do?

The mummy was almost at the entrance to the pyramid now—getting closer and closer—

Then, without warning, he skidded to a stop at the entrance, flinching as a beam of sunlight touched his bandages. Draculaura tilted her head and watched closely. The mummy was desperate to follow her, but something about the sunlight was keeping him from leaving the pyramid...and if he couldn't see her, then he couldn't curse her...

Draculaura held her breath. Watched. Waited.

At last, grumbling in defeat, the mummy slunk back into the shadows of the pyramid. With a groaning *creeeeeeak*, the heavy stone door closed behind him.

"Yes!" Draculaura cheered as loudly as she

dared. Somehow, she'd managed to escape from that miserable mummy. Now she and her ghoul-friends were safe.

There was just one problem, Draculaura realized.

Where are my ghoulfriends? she wondered.

CHAPTER 6

The vast emptiness of the desert was overwhelming. The hot sun beat down on Draculaura's head, making her feel dizzy; her arms ached so much from her crazy flight that she felt like crying. But she bit back the tears. There was no time for that—not when her ghouls were missing in action.

"Clawdeen?" Draculaura called as she stepped out from behind the statue. "Frankie?"

There was no answer.

Draculaura yelled their names again. She could hear her voice echo off the stony sides of the pyramids; it seemed to spiral high into the clear blue sky.

Or maybe that was just her imagination.

Walking at a fast pace, Draculaura set off along each side of the pyramid, still calling for her ghoulfriends. Side one—nothing. Side two—nothing. Side three—nothing. Side four...

Still nothing.

At last, she was back at the front entrance to the pyramid. It was later now; she could tell because the shadows had shifted. They seemed smaller to Draculaura. *I wish Frankie were here*, she thought suddenly. *I could ask her what that means. I guess if the sun is higher in the sky...the shadows would be shorter? Maybe?*

Draculaura felt like she should've been able to figure this out—but the heat and the stress had left her feeling all fuzzy-headed.

 73

Find your ghoulfriends, she told herself. *Worry about sun and shadows later.*

Draculaura leaned against the side of the pyramid, trying to take advantage of the narrow strip of shade that was still there. There had been absolutely no sign of Frankie or Clawdeen; she'd called their names until she was completely hoarse. There was only one possible explanation.

Her ghoulfriends were stuck *inside* the pyramid.

The thought of going back inside made Draculaura shiver with fear, despite the heat of the day. No doubt that mummy was still inside, waiting... *Maybe he went back to sleep*, Draculaura thought, grasping at hope. *Maybe he's tucked back into his cozy sarcophagus, ready to snooze away the next thousand years...*

But what if he wasn't? What if he was lying in wait, ready to strike her with curses the instant she entered his eternal resting place?

Draculaura wiped her forehead, then tucked some loose strands of hair behind her ears. She had no choice—she would have to go back into that pyramid to find her ghoulfriends. She knew that they'd do the same for her.

Draculaura took a deep breath, and when she exhaled, the heat exhaustion and the ache in her arms seemed to melt away. She would rescue her ghouls—no matter what it took.

"Okay," Draculaura whispered to herself. "Let's do this."

Cre-e-e-e-e-a-k!

Draculaura froze.

The noise sent chills racing down her spine; it was the sound of rusty hinges, of scratching nails. *The mummy!* Draculaura thought. All her muscles tensed; she was poised to run—or fly—if only she could *know* that her wings could carry her through another flight—

She watched the pyramid's door with mounting dread. Any moment now, she was sure, the mummy would open it—

Suddenly, something caught Draculaura's eye. It was movement—but not at the pyramid's main entrance.

She squinted, trying to see well despite the blinding brightness of the sun. That's when Draculaura spotted a small brass rectangle, so subtly built into the pyramid that she'd never even noticed it before.

A flash of light—the door caught the sun as it swung open—

And a familiar head of hair popped out—

"Clawdeen!" Draculaura screamed. She raced over to the little door and helped her ghoulfriend climb out, then crushed Clawdeen in a massive hug. "You made it out! I was so worried! I was just about to go back in—wait—where's Frankie?"

"Right behind you," Frankie called. She held out a hand for Draculaura to grab, then warned, "Watch out for my stitches—they feel a little loose."

Oh so carefully, Clawdeen and Draculaura pulled Frankie through the itty-bitty door. Then all the ghouls celebrated their escape from the pyramid, shrieking and laughing and hugging.

"I was so worried!" Draculaura told them. "I thought you hadn't managed to escape."

"We were worried that *you* hadn't managed to escape," Clawdeen told her.

"I felt so *bad* leaving you behind with that miserable mummy," Frankie said as she gave Draculaura another hug. "We shouldn't have split up like that."

Draculaura knelt down to take a look at the brass door, which had more hieroglyphs carved onto it. "How did you ghouls even find this?" she asked in amazement. "It looks like a pet door or something!"

"That's because it is," Clawdeen replied. She knelt next to Draculaura and pushed the door open. "Come out, Nu! What are you waiting for, a formal invitation?"

The brass door swung open once more as the mummy-cat appeared.

"Nu!" Draculaura cried. "I didn't think I'd see *you* again!"

"Nu saved us," Frankie declared. "We got so lost in the pyramid..."

"Those tunnels were a total maze," Clawdeen added. "We got so twisted and turned around I didn't know how we'd ever find our way out."

"It was pretty clawesome in there, though," Frankie continued. "There was an entire chamber filled with bling—"

"*Shiiiiiny*," Clawdeen interjected.

"And another one, filled with all these bottles and vials," Frankie finished. "It was like the world's most amazing chemistry set. I would've *loved* to run some tests to see what was in them."

Nu nuzzled his head against Draculaura's shoulder as she cuddled him. "You must've been really miserable with that mean old mummy, huh?" she said. "Don't worry. You're safe now. We'll take you back to Monster High with us. Trust me, you're gonna love it! And you'll fit right in!"

Nu sweetly licked Draculaura with his scratchy pink tongue. Then, with a flick of his tail, he jumped off her lap and started galloping across the sand, scampering like a kitten instead of a five-thousand-year-old mummy-cat.

"Nu! Come back!" Drac cried. Then she turned to her ghouls. "Was it something I said?"

"Cats can be kind of fickle," Clawdeen told her. "He's been cooped up for so long. He probably just wants to be free."

"I guess so," Draculaura said—though in her heart, she was still sorry to see Nu go.

CHAPTER 7

As Nu frolicked farther and farther away, Draculaura turned back to her ghoulfriends. "Time to regroup," she announced. "Operation Find Cleo is back on."

"All right!" cheered Frankie. "So...now what?"

"One tomb down...about a billion to go," Clawdeen said. "Where should we start?"

Draculaura shielded her eyes as she stared out at the horizon. There weren't exactly a *billion*

pyramids to search…but there were definitely more than a few.

"I have no idea," Draculaura admitted. "I guess we should go to the next closest pyramid and take it from there."

Frankie held up her hands, trying to gauge the distance between the pyramids. "It looks as if the pyramids are…*hmm*…you know, it's impossible to be completely certain, not without some surveyor's instruments or measurement tools or—"

"What's your best guess?" Clawdeen interrupted her.

"I think it's that one," Frankie said, pointing at a pyramid to the left. "It looks about three-point-two-eight kilometers away…give or take."

"Then let's go," Draculaura said. "Come on—it will be like a road trip."

"Minus the road," Clawdeen joked as she dumped some sand out of her shoes.

"*Yowch!*" Draculaura cringed as she watched a stream of sand pour out of Clawdeen's shoe. "That looks painful."

"I'm thinking these platform cutouts were not the best choice for a rescue mission in the desert," Clawdeen said. Then she pushed her hair back. "It is so *hot*."

"I know," Draculaura replied, fanning herself with her hand.

"Hey," Frankie said, sounding concerned. "You're getting all pink!"

"Is my eye shadow smudged?" Draculaura asked.

"Um, not quite..." Clawdeen said with a look of concern.

"You might be getting a sunburn," Frankie told her.

"A what?" Draculaura repeated.

"A sunburn. You know," Frankie tried to explain. "The sun's ultraviolet rays can damage and even burn skin—especially delicate skin that hasn't had much exposure to the sun."

"You mean I'm getting *burned?*" Draculaura yelped. "From the *sun?*"

"Did you put on sunscream today?" asked Clawdeen.

"No! I don't exactly have a ton of experience with leaving the house during the daytime," Draculaura cried. "This is terrible. What am I going to do? I wish we'd brought some water," Draculaura said, licking her dry lips.

"Me too. I'm super parched," Clawdeen agreed. "I don't know how much more of this I can take. My hair is too thick for this kind of heat! I'm roasting here, ghouls."

"I would give anything for an iced Mummy

Mocha at the Creepeteria right now," Draculaura said longingly.

"Come on, ghouls! We can do this!" Frankie urged them. "We're, like, almost halfway there. Remember how cool and shady the last pyramid was? We can definitely chill at the next one for a little while."

"It's so far away," Clawdeen said. "And the sweaty look is *not* in right now."

"Just keep your eyes on the prize," Frankie urged her, flinging her hand out as she pointed at the pyramid. The motion wasn't much—but it was enough to make the loose stitches unravel, causing Frankie's hand to go flying across the desert! It landed with a loud *thump* at the crest of a sand dune several feet away.

"Frankie! Your hand!" Draculaura cried.

"Whoops," Frankie said sheepishly. "That was so not supposed to happen. Embarrassing!"

"You don't have to be embarrassed in front of your ghoulfriends," Draculaura assured her.

"Come on," Clawdeen said. "Let's go get your hand."

The three ghouls set off for the dune when, suddenly, a shadow fell over them.

"Clouds?" Draculaura asked excitedly, peeking up at the sky. "Maybe it's going to rain!"

But the sun was still blazing; there wasn't a single cloud in sight.

"Not clouds." Frankie gulped. "Cobra!"

Draculaura's eyes grew wide with terror as she looked straight into the glinting eyes of a king cobra! Its hood flapped menacingly as it hissed, flicking its hot-pink tongue at the ghouls.

"Don't—make—any—sudden—moves," Frankie whispered. "Just—step—back—"

"But your hand!" Draculaura said. "We have to—"

Before Draculaura could finish her sentence,

 85

the cobra twisted around. It darted forward in one fast move, ready to strike—but instead of attacking the ghouls, it grabbed Frankie's hand in its mouth!

Clawdeen pulled herself up to her full height. "How *dare* you!" she yelled at the cobra. "Hand over the hand, Snake Lips!"

"Clawdeen!" Draculaura cried. "That's a *king cobra*! Don't make it mad!"

"Make *it* mad? It made *me* mad!" Clawdeen yelled. She pushed up her sleeves, put down her head, and started charging over the sand as the cobra slithered away with Frankie's hand. But the sand on the dunes was looser than the trail; Clawdeen immediately sank down three inches as the cobra scooted away over the sand.

"Stop that snake!" Clawdeen hollered.

"We've gotta get you out of this dune first," Frankie said.

"Are you kidding?" asked Clawdeen. "Your hand—we have to go get it!"

"I don't think so," Frankie replied.

Draculaura and Clawdeen stared at her.

"Frankie," Draculaura began. "Your *hand*—"

"We can't get it back now," Frankie pointed out. "That snake was practically designed to slither through the desert. Us? Not so much. Let's face it, ghouls: We've had better days."

"But—" Clawdeen said.

"Seriously," Frankie insisted. "You're stuck in the sand, Draculaura's burning up, and I'm practically dying of thirst. How much worse is this going to get? We can't use the rest of our energy just trying to get my hand back from that sneaky snake. I'm sure I can figure something out later."

"Frankie has a point," Draculaura said slowly. "What if we go back to Monster High and figure out what to do next? Are you okay with that, Frankie?"

"Definitely," Frankie said. "I need to recharge too. Besides, that cobra is leaving a very distinctive trail through the sand. I think we'll be able to follow it and find my hand—just as soon as we get back."

Draculaura held out the Skullette pendant. "The quicker we go, the quicker we get back."

Frankie and Clawdeen reached out and placed their fingers on the Skullette too.

"*Monster High*," the ghouls announced. "*Exsto monstrum.*"

Whoosh.

The sun, the sand, the pyramids—even the desert disappeared into a swirling vortex of blackness. Draculaura squeezed her eyes shut tight. She never thought she'd feel this way, but she couldn't *wait* to get home.

CHAPTER 8

Moments later, the ghouls materialized in the middle of Monster High's library. Dracula was so startled to see them that he leaped up from his chair, knocking over a whole stack of books waiting to be shelved.

"You're back!" he exclaimed. "I was so worried—but you made it! Hey—where's Cleo de Nile? Frankie! What happened to your hand? Ghouls—are you okay?"

"Uh…" Clawdeen began.

"We're *thirsty*," Draculaura replied. "I don't suppose the Creepeteria is open yet?"

"Not officially...but I think we can make special arrangements for you ghouls," Dracula said with a twinkle in his eyes. "Follow me!"

The ghouls dragged themselves down the hall to the Creepeteria, where they kicked off their shoes and sprawled out on the long benches while Dracula disappeared into the kitchen.

"*Ahh*," Draculaura said. "It's so *cool* in here."

"And dark," Frankie sighed.

"I could take a nap right here," Clawdeen added. "Except for all that banging. What is your dad doing, Drac?"

Draculaura shrugged. "No idea," she replied. "Maybe he's testing out the new coffinccino machine!"

Sure enough, Dracula soon hurried into the Creepeteria, carrying a tray with three tall iced coffinccinos. The ghouls grabbed them eagerly;

Draculaura had never tasted anything so good before!

Then Dracula put a pitcher of ice water on the table. "Drink some of this too," he said. "You don't want to get dehydrated."

"Thanks, Dad," Draculaura said gratefully. "This is just what we needed."

"Tell me everything," he replied. "You arrived in the desert...then what?"

The ghouls took turns telling him about everything that had happened after the Monster Mapalogue had dropped them in the middle of the desert.

"We didn't really want to leave Frankie's hand behind, of course," Draculaura explained. "But we were all fading fast. It was *not* a pretty sight."

"You did the right thing," Dracula told them.

"Besides, we're going right back," Clawdeen said. "As soon as everybody's rested and refreshed."

Draculaura watched her father carefully. How would he react to Clawdeen's announcement? Would he say it was too dangerous? Would he forbid them to use the Monster Mapalogue again?

"Well, of course you are," Dracula said. "And when you go back, you'll be ready."

Then, with a mysterious smile—and not another word—he left the Creepeteria.

The ghouls looked at one another in confusion.

"What was that about?" asked Frankie.

Clawdeen took another sip of her drink. "Maybe he's going to make another round of coffinccinos," she said. "I could definitely use a double."

"I'm not so sure," Draculaura replied, deep in thought.

The ghouls turned to look at her.

"Maybe Dad is trying to tell us we need to *really* be ready for Operation Find Cleo," she continued. "Not just charge off into the desert without a plan, you know?"

 92

"What kind of plan are you talking about?" asked Frankie.

"I don't know," Draculaura admitted. She held out her arms. "But think about where we are— Monster High! The very first fully equipped high school for monsters, beasties, and ghouls of all kinds. We've got everything except…"

"Students?" guessed Clawdeen.

"Exactly—which means Monster High is ready to go!" Draculaura exclaimed. "We can *learn* everything we need to know to survive in the desert—and how to make Operation Find Cleo a success."

For a moment, the other ghouls didn't say anything.

Then Frankie started slowly nodding. "I like it," she said. "I like it a lot!"

"I'll get started in the Howl of History," Draculaura said. "How about you, Frankie?"

"The Mad Science lab," Frankie said right away.

 93

Then she turned to Clawdeen. "Where will you go, Clawdeen?"

"I'm not sure yet," Clawdeen said. "I guess I'll just...wander around a little until I figure out where to do my research."

"Let's meet back at the library in an hour," Draculaura said excitedly. "See you ghouls soon!"

Draculaura raced through the halls of Monster High so fast that she skidded on the polished floor and almost missed the Howl of History. Luckily, Webby was near; he shot out a sticky strand of spiderweb and caught her tight.

"Thanks, Webby." Draculaura giggled as she pulled the web out of her hair. Then she stepped into the history classroom, closed the door, and took a deep breath. The smell of the classroom alone was enough to make her even more excited about Monster High's grand opening—it was a mixture of freshly sharpened pencils, the creased parchment of ancient books of monster lore, and a wall-size, weathered map of the entire monster world. With a large leather globe and five hundred volumes of the Monsterpedia lining the walls, Draculaura knew that she'd come to the perfect place for her research.

Now—where to begin?

Draculaura started to spin the globe—slowly at first, then faster and faster. Places flew by in a blur: Germany, Hawaii, Mexico, New York, Madrid.

We've got a lot of pyramids waiting for us, she thought, spinning the globe until her index finger rested on Egypt. *Maybe there's something in here that can help me narrow down where we might find Cleo.*

As if on cue, sparks started flying from the spinning globe. Draculaura jumped back in alarm—then leaned closer in amazement. It was almost as if the globe was trying to tell her something.

The Monster Mapalogue, she thought suddenly. *Maybe it's not the only thing that can help us find Cleo!*

"Cleo," Draculaura said aloud, her voice echoing in the empty room. "I need to find Cleo."

The globe spun back around to Egypt; dozens of three-dimensional pyramids popped up on the globe's surface. One of them seemed taller and brighter than the others...but how would Draculaura find that particular pyramid when she was back in the middle of the desert?

The globe was crackling now, with bright lines of electricity forming a web across it. Cautiously, carefully, Draculaura reached out and gently touched the tip of the largest pyramid. It seemed to tremble—the whole *room* seemed to tremble—and then a number materialized in the air: 3912.

Three thousand nine hundred and twelve? Draculaura wondered. *What does* that *mean?*

Was the number connected to Cleo? Was it the square footage of her pyramid? How old she was?

The number of creeperific accessories stashed away in her tomb?

"Okay, maybe not that last one," Draculaura said out loud.

Then her gaze drifted over to all the Monster-pedia volumes lining the wall—and inspiration struck.

Draculaura hurried over to the bookshelves and started flipping through each volume. It wasn't until she reached #42 that she found page 3,912—and an entry on Cleo!

Cleo De Nile

A famed princess of Egypt, Cleo de Nile is renowned for her high style and regal presence. The daughter of Ramses de Nile, Princess Cleo is the latest in a long line of Egyptian royalty. She never settles for second best—no matter what.

Draculaura paused reading only long enough to pull out her iCoffin, where she started taking notes as fast as she could. Draculaura even snapped a pic of Cleo's custom hieroglyphs.

Cleo loves gold—and that's exactly what this info is, Draculaura thought gleefully. *Golden!*

Meanwhile, Frankie made her way to the underground lab where Monster High's Mad Science classes would be held. Since she'd grown up in a lab, hiding out near a power station, Frankie felt at home the moment she stepped inside Monster High's lab.

"Voltageous!" Frankie cried as she ran into the lab, which was as silent as an underground tomb. Except for one sound...

Plink.

Plink.

Plink.

Frankie listened carefully as she tried to figure out where the sound was coming from. Everything in the lab was brand new; all the equipment looked as if it had never been used before. There were long steel counters for workspaces and five different cabinets filled with beakers, flasks, and test tubes. As Frankie explored, she discovered a massive storage cupboard filled with every element and chemical she'd ever heard of—and even some that she hadn't. The lab had everything she could ever imagine needing to—

Frankie paused; a look of deep consideration crossed her face. *What am I going to do here?* she wondered. *What's the best way that I can help Operation Find Cleo be a shocking success?*

Plink.

Plink.

Plink.

There was that noise again.

Where's that sound coming from? Frankie

wondered. She explored the lab a little more and found a section of safety gear that had been completely blinged out: studded lab coats with monsterrific designs and goggles that dazzled with rhinestones. There was even a selection of hair accessories in every color imaginable so that ghouls could coordinate with their outfits when they tied back their long hair.

Draculaura planned for everything, Frankie thought with a grin. *Safety first doesn't mean fashion last!*

With all those chemicals and elements, Frankie could try to brew a potion—but what *kind* of potion? "Some kind of sunscream would be good for Draculaura," she mused. "Actually, it would be good for all of us to lotion up before we head back to the desert."

But Frankie wanted to do more to help in the rescue efforts. She paced around the lab, deep in thought, as she examined all the different supplies and materials at her disposal. Frankie

 100

had been a fiend for chemistry ever since she got her very first chemistry set, which she'd used to reanimate a dead caterpillar so that it could transform into a zombie butterfly. Her dad had never been more proud!

But that kind of science wasn't exactly useful right now...or was it?

Plink.

Plink.

Plink.

That noise is driving me crazy! Frankie frowned as the strange sound distracted her again. *First things first*, she decided. *I'm going to find out what's making that noise, then figure out a brilliant idea to make our mission a surefire success.*

Frankie roamed the entire lab until, at last, she discovered a sink at the very back of the room. Sure enough, the faucet wasn't turned off enough; it was drip-drip-dripping, and each drop of water hit the steel sink with a resounding *plink.*

Frankie twisted the faucet to stop the dripping, then smiled in silence. *Peace and quiet...at last!* she thought. *Now if only it were so easy to find water in the deserts of Egypt...*

Frankie glanced across the room and discovered a large steel box that had been bolted to the wall. A familiar symbol on it captured her attention: HIGH VOLTAGE.

A smile spread across Frankie's face as the bolts in her neck started sparking. She had found water, all right.

And that gave her a brilliant idea.

Clawdeen wandered through the halls of Monster High until she reached the arts wing. She had a funny feeling that this was where all her favorite classes would be. After all, her own mother would be teaching art class. A passion for the arts definitely ran in Clawdeen's family.

Clawdeen glanced at the music room, a bright, airy space under the rafters. There weren't any monsters using the music room, but it was far from silent; Clawdeen noticed a hornets' nest in the eaves that was bustling with activity.

Ugh, she thought, glad that the hornets were way up high—and not paying any attention to her.

As Clawdeen explored, she found drawers and drawers of haunting music from all over the monster world and more instruments than she had ever seen before. A set of small chimes hung from the ceiling; Clawdeen touched them with her finger. A spooky series of notes materialized and began to float through the air, and then the notes themselves began to play other instruments! Clawdeen had never seen anything like it.

But it was how the musical notes affected the hornets that really captured Clawdeen's attention. As the music notes filled the room, the hornets stopped buzzing. They hovered above their hive, silent and transfixed by the gentle tones of the notes. Clawdeen had never seen drowsy hornets before, but she knew that's exactly what these hornets now were—very sleepy!

That is so *clawesome*, Clawdeen thought.

The unusual powers of the chimes gave Clawdeen an idea. Was it a creepy-crazy one? Definitely.

But that meant it just might work!

An hour later, all three ghouls met back at the library.

"You will not even believe how much I learned about Cleo," Draculaura raved. "I can't wait to meet her!"

"Here, ghouls," Frankie said as she passed a tube of thick white paste to them. "I made you some sunscream. Gotta take care of your skin!"

"What's that?" Clawdeen asked, pointing at a silver stick-like thing that Frankie had tucked under her arm.

"You'll see," Frankie said mysteriously. "I don't want to spoil the big surprise."

"Monsterously mysterious!" giggled Draculaura. Then she turned to Clawdeen. "What did you learn?"

"You know how they say that music has charms to soothe the savage beastie?" asked Clawdeen.

Draculaura and Frankie nodded.

"Well, you are not gonna *believe* what it does for hornets!" Clawdeen announced. She held up a suede pouch and shook it so that the fringe dangling from it danced back and forth.

"I'm confused—you're going to tickle it to death with fringe?" guessed Frankie.

Clawdeen's eyes twinkled. "Even better," she replied. "And that's all I'm going to say."

"So many spooky secrets," Draculaura said, shaking her head. "If you two won't spill until we get back to the desert, then I guess we'd better get going!"

She held out the Skullette. By now, everyone knew the drill.

"*Cleo. Exsto monstrum.*"

Whoosh!

CHAPTER 9

The Monster Mapalogue brought the ghouls back to the exact same location in the desert where they'd been before. Draculaura noticed right away that the sun had shifted a lot; they'd been gone only a couple hours, but it made a huge difference in the heat index. Even better, the cobra's tracks were still clearly visible in the sand!

"What's that?" asked Frankie, pointing at some odd-looking indentations in the sand nearby. "Looks like some kind of tracks."

"There's only one track I'm interested in," Draculaura said, pointing to the curving line that stretched through the sand. "The one that leads to Frankie's hand. Clawdeen, you want to clue us in to your plan?"

"And ruin the surprise?" Clawdeen joked. "Don't worry, ghouls, I got this. Prepare to be amazed!"

Draculaura was so excited as the ghouls traipsed across the dunes. "See, this? *This?* This is *exactly* why we needed Monster High!" she exclaimed. "I mean, in just one hour we learned so much. Imagine what it's going to be like when all the teachers and students arrive!"

"It's going to be totally clawesome—that's what it's going to be," Clawdeen replied.

"And best of all, we won't have to hide any-more," Draculaura said. "Monsters coming out of the shadows; monsters coming out of all the lonely and forgotten hiding places of the world. I mean, when we put all our skills and talents and smarts together—we're going to be unstoppable!"

"But that was one of the problems, wasn't it?" Frankie pointed out.

"What do you mean?" Draculaura asked her.

"That's why humans came after us—because they were scared of us," Frankie explained. "And you know what that led to."

"The great monster Fright Flight," Clawdeen said in a solemn voice.

"Exactly," Frankie said.

"But it doesn't have to be like that," Draculaura insisted. "I mean, sure, maybe Dad's right and monsters need to lay low for a while…just until humans get used to the idea of us. But that doesn't mean we all have to be apart…afraid…alone."

"It's true—Monster High is going to change *everything*," Clawdeen said. "And I, for one, can't wait. Like when you see what I learned in the music classroom…"

"Yeah? Well, now's your chance," Frankie said. "Because I think we've found what we were looking for."

With her remaining hand, Frankie pointed to the hollow of one of the dunes, where the king cobra had made a sandy nest filled with snake eggs—all of them guarded by Frankie's lost hand!

"Frankie! It's your hand!" Draculaura cried. "And I don't see that slimy snake anywhere! Come on, let's run up and grab it. We'll go back to the pyramids, get our ghoul Cleo, and be home in time for dinner. I don't know about you ghouls but I'm really hungry! We should have fueled up when—"

Hissssssssssssssssssssssssssssssss!

Without warning, the cobra suddenly popped out of a small hole in the sand. It leaned over the ghouls, menacing them as it spread out its hood. All the ghouls screamed!

"I take it back!" Draculaura squeaked. "You're not slimy at all. In fact, I think you're remarkably clean, considering there's no water here."

The snake, though, only got angrier.

"Step aside, ghouls," Clawdeen announced. "I got this."

She reached into the suede pouch and pulled out a set of small, hollow tubes that gleamed under the desert sun. They reminded Draculaura of wind chimes—until Clawdeen started screwing them together.

"Distract my slithering friend for a moment, would you?" Clawdeen asked.

"Uh...how?" asked Frankie.

"I don't know, sing a song or something," Clawdeen replied.

Draculaura made a face. Serenading a snake did not sound like the solution right now.

Frankie's bolts started blinking. "I have a voltageous idea," she said as she held up the silver

 111

stick she'd made in the lab. "Hey, Desert Breath!" she called. "Go fetch!"

Then Frankie threw the stick with all of her might. It tumbled through the air, glittering in the sunshine, until it landed in the sand, standing straight up.

The cobra, however, was supremely unimpressed. He raised himself higher, casting a looming shadow over the three ghouls.

"Uh—Clawdeen?" Draculaura whispered. "We have a situation here!"

"Almost...ready..." Clawdeen said, her forehead furrowed in concentration. "Yes! Got it!"

Clawdeen held up her hand in triumph. She was holding some sort of instrument; Draculaura had never seen anything like it before. It was like a cross between a flute, a harmonica, and a set of wind chimes. Clawdeen's secret weapon was not at all what Draculaura was expecting.

The king cobra began weaving back and forth, fervently guarding its lair...and Frankie's hand.

"Ghouls! I think he's getting ready to strike!" Frankie whispered urgently.

"You're...sure this is going to work?" Draculaura asked Clawdeen.

"Here's hoping," Clawdeen replied. She brought the instrument to her mouth and began to play a boo-tiful melody. Each note echoed, seamlessly merging into the next one, until the air seemed to quiver with music. Shimmering notes materialized in the air and surrounded the cobra; Draculaura grabbed Frankie's arm and watched in amazement as the snake's eyelids began to droop...and then its head began to drop...

"Are you seeing this?" Frankie asked in a low voice. "It's getting sleepy..."

"Very sleepy..." added Draculaura.

Clawdeen, still playing, managed to give the

ghouls a thumbs-up. The snake sighed—a heavy, drowsy sound—and curled itself into a tight coil, nestling its head on its scaly skin.

The ghouls held their breath as the last note of Clawdeen's song hung in the air, then faded into nothingness.

"Okay," Frankie whispered. "I'm gonna go get my hand."

"Wait," Draculaura said. "Let me go."

"But—" Frankie began.

Draculaura didn't let her finish. "Come on, that's what ghoulfriends are for," she said. "Besides, if any of your other stitches get loose..."

"I see your point," Frankie admitted. "Thanks, Drac. Just be careful!"

Draculaura gave Frankie's arm a quick squeeze, then crept forward as silently as she could. The only sound was the almost imperceptible *crunch-crunch-crunch* of dry sand under her hot-pink lace-up shoes.

Draculaura was just inches from the cobra's nest. All she had to do was reach over the sleeping snake and pluck Frankie's hand from the pile of shiny eggs...

Almost...got...it... Draculaura thought, her face contorted with effort as she reached— reached—reached—

HISSSSSSSSSSSSSSSSSSSSSS!

Without warning, the snake awoke—in an even worse mood! It raised up to its full height and hovered over Draculaura; she could see a drop of venom glistening on the tip of its fang. Draculaura tried to get away, but the sand slipped beneath her feet—she wobbled and fell—

"Clawdeen!" Frankie shrieked. "Play your song again!"

"Too late for that," Clawdeen growled. In an instant, she went full-on werewolf, using her superspeed and superstrength to leap protectively in front of Draculaura. Then Clawdeen threw back her head and roared so loudly that the ground shook!

The cobra took one look at the terrifying werewolf towering over it and shrank back down. Then it slithered away as fast as its scales could go!

The three ghouls jumped into the air, shrieking and cheering as Draculaura rescued Frankie's hand from the nest of snake eggs.

"Clawdeen! I didn't know you could do that!" Draculaura exclaimed. "That was fangtastic!"

Clawdeen shrugged as if it were no big deal, but her proud smile gave away how pleased she was. "It's nothing, just a thing I used to do when my brothers got out of hand," she said. "Works every time!"

"Quick, give me my hand," Frankie said. "Because I want to high-five *both* of you ghouls!"

CHAPTER 10

Next stop—Cleo!" Draculaura announced.

"Not so fast," Frankie spoke up. "We've gotta stay hydrated, remember? We've been back in the desert for an hour already."

"Yeah," Clawdeen agreed as she pulled back her thick hair. "That iced coffinccino is a distant memory."

"I totally agree. Ancient history—just like that mummy we escaped earlier." Draculaura giggled. Then she turned to Frankie. "You're so right, ghoul. We can't get all droopy and draggy again—we still have to find Cleo! So how are we going to refresh out here?"

"Now that I've got both hands, I can show you exactly how my invention works!" Frankie said. She hurried across the sandy dunes to retrieve the silver stick. "*Ooh*—almost too hot to handle," she said, passing the stick from one hand to the other.

"Who would've thought gloves would be the must-have accessory for desert heat?" joked Draculaura.

"Frankie, how is that stick going to help us find water?" Clawdeen asked.

"Well, it's not a regular stick, for one thing," Frankie said, her eyes shining as she held up her invention proudly. "I did some research and figured out that there's a way to find water underground. I invented this special stick that can be waved over the ground to pick up the presence of minerals that would be present only near a water source. When the stick detects these minerals, it will vibrate because of what's in the core of the stick, and this is where it gets really exciting... are you ghouls listening?"

"Sorry, Frankie," Draculaura said sheepishly. "But as long as your invention works, that's good enough for me!"

Frankie rubbed her hands together until she formed a crackling electrical charge; then, with both hands, she held her invention over the ground.

"Now I know you ghouls already know that water and electricity *don't* mix—but stand back, okay?" Frankie called out.

Draculaura and Clawdeen took an extra-big step backward—just in case.

The silver stick jerked Frankie forward for several steps; it looked like it took all her strength to hold onto it. Then, just as abruptly, it stopped short.

"Yes!" Frankie cheered. "There should be water...right...here!"

She twirled her invention around in her hands like a glittering baton, then—*bam!* Frankie plunged it into the sand.

Suddenly—*whoosh!* A massive jet of water sprang up from the ground, creating a cool fountain in the middle of the desert.

Draculaura and Clawdeen shrieked as the fountain sprayed cool mist over them.

"Yes!" exclaimed Frankie with a triumphant fist pump. "It works!"

"Works? That's an understatement!" Draculaura cried as she spun around in the fountain's spray. "I mean, that was *fangtastic!*"

"Truly clawesome," added Clawdeen as she slicked back her hair.

The ghouls danced around in the desert fountain, then drank their fill of the cold, clear water. When everyone felt completely refreshed and recharged, Frankie pulled her invention out of the sand; the fountain slowed to a trickle as the sand scattered across it.

"All right—back to business," Draculaura said. "We've got to figure out which pyramid belongs to Cleo."

"So...we're right back where we were before," Clawdeen said.

"Not quite," Draculaura told her as she whipped out her iCoffin. "I did a little research in the history classroom and learned a *ton* about Cleo."

"Like what?" asked Frankie.

"First, remember what Cleo said in her message," Draculaura reminded her ghouls. "She was stuck and had a score to settle."

Frankie cringed. "I think we should try to avoid getting in the middle of a mummy brawl," she said.

"Yeah...I agree," Draculaura said. "I hope we can convince Cleo that this whole cursing thing is just bad luck. And when she comes to Monster

High, there will be so many cool things to do that she'll forget all about settling scores and cursing others."

"So what else did you learn about her?" asked Clawdeen.

"Well, Cleo's not just a ghoul—she's also a princess," Draculaura said as she ticked each tidbit off on her fingers. "Actual royalty! And apparently, Cleo's love of bling is legendary."

"That might be useful," Clawdeen responded.

"The Monsterpedia said that Cleo's entire existence revolved around luxury," Draculaura told the other ghouls. "So—maybe her final resting place does too."

"Are you thinking what I'm thinking?" asked Frankie.

"Find the fanciest pyramid and take it from there?" guessed Draculaura.

"Exactly! High-five!" Frankie said. She held up her newly attached hand for yet another high five. "Sorry." She giggled. "It's just so good to have my hand back."

"That's great info and all—but all the pyramids look the same from the outside," Clawdeen pointed out. "We're still gonna have to explore each one until we find the pyramid with the most bling."

"Maybe not," Draculaura said as she rummaged around in her pocket and pulled out a set of tiny antique binoculars she'd found in the Howl of History. She brought the binoculars up to her face and peered through them, carefully examining each distant pyramid.

"Ghouls!" Draculaura cried in excitement. "The pyramids—they're *not* all the same!"

"Really?" asked Frankie.

"Let me see!" Clawdeen demanded.

Draculaura passed the binoculars over to Clawdeen, who gasped as soon as she glanced through them.

"They only look the same from a distance," Clawdeen reported as she passed the binoculars to Frankie.

"That's voltageous!" Frankie marveled.

Draculaura took the binoculars again. "It looks like each one is a slightly different color," she said. "I bet they used to be really bright a long time ago."

"They've probably been bleached by the sun," Frankie mused.

"But that one—way over on the right side—see it? It's kind of shiny—it *gleams* almost," Draculaura said.

Frankie took another turn with the binoculars. "You know what?" she said slowly. "I think that pyramid might actually be made of...gold bricks."

"Seriously?" asked Draculaura.

"Yeah," Frankie said, nodding. "Gold is one of the softer metals—and you can kind of see how the bricks are pitted, like from centuries of sand-storms. And—what's that on top? Some sort of jewel?"

Draculaura glanced through the binoculars. "It's a jeweled scarab—just like the one Cleo was wearing in her message!" She gasped.

The three ghouls exchanged a glance. They all knew what *that* meant.

"Well, what are we waiting for? Let's go get our ghoul!" Clawdeen finally cried.

The ghouls set off for the golden pyramid. As the sun began to set, the pyramid glimmered even more, as if spangled with beams of red and orange light. But nothing they'd seen in the desert was nearly as breathtaking as the doors to the golden pyramid: Bejeweled with precious gems in every color of the rainbow, they glittered invitingly.

"I like this ghoul's style," Draculaura said approvingly. "Come on—let's open these doors."

 125

"Don't you think it's kind of weird that nobody's stolen these jewels?" asked Frankie. "I mean, they're right here, out in the open."

Clawdeen threw her arms out and gestured to the empty desert. "Who would steal them?" she asked. "We're the only ones around for miles and miles."

Draculaura knelt down and pulled a few long grayish threads off the facets of a ruby. "Someone *has* been here," she reported. "But they left the jewels behind."

Clawdeen shrugged, then pushed up her sleeves and flexed her muscles. "After the doors to the last pyramid, I'm ready to put some muscle into it," she joked.

The other ghouls got into position next to Clawdeen and prepared to push open the heavy door. Draculaura braced herself for the earsplitting *creeeeeak* of the ancient door's wheels grinding against the track.

 126

But to her surprise, the door slid open easily, gliding along the track until the entrance to the pyramid was open wide. The floor seemed to be covered with gleaming black tiles—but they weren't straight and even. *That's weird,* Draculaura thought as she looked at the uneven floor. *I thought Cleo wouldn't settle for second best. But whoever paved this floor did a terrible job.*

Suddenly, Draculaura realized that the floor was *moving.*

It took a few more moments for Draculaura's eyes to adjust to the dim light—but when they did, she suddenly understood everything: why the floor was uneven and why it wouldn't stay still.

What lurked inside the pyramid was worse than the ghouls ever could've imagined.

CHAPTER 11

Ghouls," Draculaura whispered. "Are you seeing this?"

"Unfortunately, yes," Frankie replied.

"And I thought the king cobra was bad," Clawdeen added.

The truth was, none of the girls knew what the floor of the pyramid *really* looked like—because it was carpeted with an army of jet-black, hard-shelled scorpions! Hundreds—thousands—*millions* of them. Even as the scorpions snoozed, their barbed tails arched up, ready to strike if they were disturbed.

The worst part wasn't how many scorpions there were. It wasn't even their barbed stingers. No, it was the fact that after all they'd done, after all they'd been through, the scorpions were standing between the ghouls and Cleo.

"Check that out," Clawdeen said in a low voice, pointing to two torches that blazed on the far side of the pyramid. There was a door between them, marked with the same glittering scarab jewel that graced the top of the pyramid. "Bet you Cleo's in there."

"But how are we gonna get past *them?*" Frankie asked, pointing at the scorpion army.

"Think, think, think," Draculaura said, pressing her fingers into her temples as she racked her brain. "There's *got* to be a way. Clawdeen, what if— no— or Frankie—but—"

"Ghoul, I mean this in the nicest possible way,

but you're not making any sense," Clawdeen said. "You want to try finishing those sentences?"

"It's just—all the scorpions are asleep right now," Draculaura whispered. "I was thinking maybe there is a way we could use your instrument and Frankie's invention to get past them— but if it doesn't work, and we wake them and they're all cranky and sting-y—"

"Yeah," Clawdeen said. "I see your point."

"I *wish* I had done more research into the beasties of Egypt," Draculaura groaned.

"You want to go home?" asked Frankie. "We could spend the rest of the night researching scorpions and try again tomorrow."

"But we're so close!" Draculaura cried. "I just want to get Cleo and get out of here! Not let everybody down."

Frankie put her arm around Drac's shoulders. "Don't talk like that, ghoulfriend," she began.

Ker-plink.

Everyone froze as the delicate chain holding the Skullette snapped. The Skullette plunged to the floor, landing with such a clatter that the sound echoed throughout the tomb!

The scorpions stirred, shifted, swelled like a shiny black wave—

Draculaura lunged for the Skullette, but it was too late. The scorpions were awake—and they didn't seem happy about it. They swarmed over the Skullette as they charged toward the ghouls.

"Up here!" Clawdeen yelled as she climbed onto a crumbling marble pillar. She held her hands out to help Draculaura and Frankie up too. Draculaura had failed to retrieve the Skullette, but at least the ghouls were safe.

For now.

"This is bad," Frankie said. "Like really, seriously bad."

"How are we going to get out of this one without getting a bunch of scorpion stings?" Clawdeen asked.

"I don't know," Draculaura replied. "I can't even *see* the Skullette anymore! It's buried under a blanket of scorpions."

Clawdeen shuddered. "Ugh! The worst!" she said.

"Um, ghouls?" Draculaura said suddenly. "Scorpions can't *climb*, can they?"

Frankie peered over the edge of the pillar. "Actually, now that you mention it, it looks like they can," she reported.

That was it—the final straw. All three ghouls screamed!

Suddenly, a bandaged blur flew past them. At first, Draculaura thought it was a bird—or a bat—but that wasn't quite right. She squinted. Whatever the thing was, it looked awfully familiar.

"Ghouls!" she shrieked. "It's Nu! Mummy-cat Nu is here!"

"Nu! He must've been following us!" Frankie exclaimed. "The weird trail in the sand—the bandage threads on the door—"

"Even better, he's pouncing on all the scorpions!" reported Clawdeen.

Draculaura could barely believe it was true. But sure enough, Nu was leaping and jumping, pouncing on the scorpions and tossing them high into the air. The ghouls cheered for the mummy-cat, who was clearly having the best day of his life.

Soon Nu had cleared enough space for the ghouls to climb down from the pillar. The moment they were on the floor, Draculaura grabbed the Skullette. At least now the ghouls would have a way to get back to Monster High!

Meanwhile, Frankie charged up her invention and used it to scatter the scorpions, who seemed to be scared of its crackling electrical bolts. Then Clawdeen started playing her instrument. The scorpions closest to her calmed down immediately. It took several minutes, but soon there was a clear path across the diamond-paved floor—a path that led directly to the torch-lit scarab door.

"Go, Drac, go!" Frankie called. Clawdeen didn't stop playing for a moment as she gestured, urging Draculaura onward.

Draculaura took a deep breath and steeled herself. *You got this,* she thought, giving herself a little pep talk. *Nu has the scorpions under control. And who cares about some scorpions when your new ghoulfriend is waiting for you—right on the other side of that door?*

With careful steps, Draculaura made her way through the tomb, leaping over any rogue scorpions that tried to scuttle across her path. Nu was definitely doing a good job of scaring off the scorpions. The few that remained seemed to want to avoid Draculaura as much as she wanted to avoid them! Then—she could hardly believe it—she had arrived.

"I'm coming, Cleo!" Draculaura hollered as she pushed against the scarab door.

But it didn't budge.

Draculaura tried again.

Again, the door didn't move.

"Ghouls!" she yelled over her shoulder. "I need you. The door won't open!"

Draculaura stood back to examine the door. She couldn't see any locks or obstacles that prevented it from opening. And there was plenty of light back here; the two torches burned steadily, casting a flickering glow and perfuming the air with the scent of honey.

Honey...Draculaura thought—and a new idea struck her. She reached up to touch the bottom edge of the torch. Its nubby surface left a sticky residue on her fingers.

"Beeswax!" she shrieked.

"Huh?" Frankie and Clawdeen said at the same time.

Draculaura turned to face them, beaming. "The torches are made from beeswax," she said eagerly. "You know, like for candles? And I think that as they've been burning for the past millennium or so, they've been dripping along the edge of the door—sealing it shut! See?"

Draculaura reached up to the golden edge of the door and dug at it with her fingers. It took a couple minutes, but eventually she pried out a chunk of crystallized honey. And that wasn't all—

A shaft of light spilled through the hole Draculaura had made!

"Come on, ghouls—dig!" she cried.

Frankie, Clawdeen, and Draculaura started scraping out the thick honey and beeswax that had sealed the door shut. As they did, more and more light spilled out from around the door. At last, every chunk of honey had been removed.

"Good work, ghouls," Clawdeen said. Then she examined her nails with a slight frown. "I am definitely going to need a manicure when we get back to Monster High. Totally worth it, though!"

"Let's get this door open," Draculaura said. Then she paused. "Or—I guess we could knock first."

"Go for it," Frankie said.

Draculaura made a fist and knocked three times on the door. The metallic echo rang through the tomb.

Then she stood back and waited.

At first, nothing.

All of a sudden, the sound of gears creaking and clanking filled the tomb. A trapdoor slid open in the floor as a golden staircase raised up from the depths of the pyramid. A series of spotlights began to flash as clouds of smoke filled the room.

Then the door opened.

An elegant ghoul struck a pose in the doorway.

She had jet-black hair with gleaming gold high-lights, and her blue eyes were the same color as her embroidered tunic. Gold bangles clinked around her wrists, a perfect complement to her gold chandelier earrings. Even the bandages she wore wrapped around one arm and leg were the height of fashion.

"You're here!" she cried.

"You must be Cleo!" Draculaura exclaimed.

"The one and only!" Cleo declared, posing again. Then she hurried down the stairs and hugged her new ghoulfriends.

"I'm Drac, this is Frankie, and over there is Clawdeen," Draculaura explained.

"Thank you so much for coming to get me!" Cleo said. "I chose those beeswax candles for aromatherapy purposes but let me tell you, *never* again. I have been stuck in there for *ages*; it was the *worst*."

The ghouls peeked around Cleo to see an amazing crypt that was tricked out with the latest in luxury.

"Looks pretty clawesome to me," Clawdeen said.

Cleo waved her hand in the air. "Oh, yes, it's golden and all, but after a few thousand years, a ghoul needs a change of scenery, you know? Plus, the reception was *terrible*. I could barely get a signal on my iCoffin."

"Yeah, we had a little trouble receiving your message," Draculaura told her. "And, actually, we're hoping you'll come back to Monster High with us. It's going to be a fresh start for everybody—no more hiding, no more loneliness. And no need to settle any scores, right?"

Cleo looked confused. "Settle any scores? What are you talking about?"

Now it was Draculaura's turn to be confused. "Your message—you said we'd need to settle the score," she reminded Cleo.

"*Ohhhh,*" Cleo said, a grin spreading over her

face as she figured out what Draculaura was talking about. "No, no, no—not settle scores. Settle the scorpions. I was warning you about them! They can be kind of cranky, and you can't try to cross them unless they have been gently awoken and then settled down. So, if you didn't get my message, how did you get past them?"

"We had a little help from a friend," Frankie said. She glanced around the tomb. "Nu? Where are you?"

"Look!" Clawdeen cried. "Nu found a friend!"

Draculaura beamed as she looked over and saw two mummy-cats playing together.

"Oh yes, that's my cat, Mau," Cleo explained. "She and Nu were totally inseparable before the great monster Fright Flight—you know, before we all went into our pyramids for safety. They've been apart for way too long!"

"It looks like they're making up for lost time," Draculaura said, smiling. "Do you think Mau wants to come to Monster High too? We already asked Nu, but he wasn't interested."

Cleo paused. "I'm not sure," she said slowly. "She…seems pretty happy here with Nu."

"She's enjoying her new freedom," Frankie explained. "I think we can all relate."

"And they obviously have *plenty* of scorpions to keep them busy," Clawdeen joked.

"This Monster High—it has vacations, right?" asked Cleo as she watched Nu and Mau scamper through the pyramid. "Because I could always come back to check on them."

"Absolutely," Draculaura assured her. "And, you know, we're your Monster High Student Outreach Committee. Anything we can help with—just ask."

"Oh, *royal*!" Cleo said brightly. "It's been a *millennium* since I've had help. Now, my luggage is over there. Do be careful carrying it; those jewels are on loan from the pharaoh."

Cleo pointed at one of the walls of her chamber. Gold trunks were stacked one on top of another, forming a massive pyramid that stretched almost to the ceiling.

"Um…I'm afraid there won't be room for all that stuff at the Monster High dorms," Draculaura said, choosing her words carefully. "But don't worry, we've got all the basics!"

"A personal chef," Cleo said, relieved.

"No—but there's a great Creepeteria…" Draculaura replied.

"Okay…how about a royal masseuse?" Cleo asked hopefully.

The other ghouls shook their heads.

"Surely you have a ruby-encrusted lounging throne?" Cleo continued.

One look at the other ghouls' faces told her all she needed to know. Cleo sighed—but her disappointment lasted only a moment. "At least I finally have friends," she said as she grinned happily at

Draculaura, Frankie, and Clawdeen. "When can we leave?"

"How about...right now?" Draculaura said.

The ghouls said good-bye to Nu and Mau, then walked through the pyramid, now empty of scorpions. As soon as they got outside, Draculaura's iCoffin started beeping. "Three missed messages!" she exclaimed.

"I told you the reception was terrible in there," Cleo said.

The ghouls gathered around Draculaura as she played her voice mail.

"Draculaura! Ghoulfriend!" a voice with an Australian accent said. "This is Lagoona Blue. I'm from Down Under and would love to come to Monster High. It sounds totally fintastic! Can you help me? It is so *washed up* here! Thanks, mates!"

Draculaura looked at each one of her new ghoulfriends: Frankie first, then Clawdeen, and last—but definitely not least—Cleo.

"What do you ghouls think?" Draculaura asked. "Ready for another adventure?"

"Voltageous!" Frankie cried.

"Clawesome!" Clawdeen said.

"Golden!" added Cleo.

All four ghouls placed their fingertips on the Skullette...

WELCOME TO
MONSTER 💀 HIGH™

Read the full fangtastic story of how Draculaura
and her ghoulfriends started Monster High in
WELCOME TO MONSTER HIGH!
Turn the page for a sneak peek!

Chapter 1

Midnight at Monster High

Alarm clocks were ringing, sleepy students were yawning, and another normal night at Monster High was about to begin. But as Draculaura always says, "*Normal* is relative."

The alarm clock was shaped like a skull. The hand that hit the snooze button wasn't a hand at all. It was a tentacle! A beastie named Woolee staggered into her bathroom to brush her tusks with a giant kitchen broom. Elsewhere, muddy water sprayed out of a rusty showerhead. A swamp monster happily scrubbed the thorny vines of his hair.

Claws and flippers were opening re-odorant,

checking lipstick, and unscrewing tubes of hair gloop. It was midnight. School was about to begin.

"Normal is about how you feel," Draculaura explained. "Not how you look or what you do."

A skeleton, Bonesy, polished his skull with a buffer in front of the mirror. His brother, Skelly, put on a pair of cool shades. Too bad he didn't have ears to hold them in place; they slipped right off his earless head.

"Normal is different for everyone," Draculaura added. She looked at the brightly colored outfit she had laid out on her bed. It didn't seem quite right. What should she wear today? She looked in her closet.

Her white miniskirt with the black netting. Her black shirt. Her pink vest. That was the look she was going for. A little Goth. A little pretty. And *all* vampire.

Monsters were sleepily headed to the Creepateria for breakfast. A piece of toast popped out of the ghoaster. An enormous mountain of cereal was disappearing from a bowl. Behind it was a gobbling glob of purple goblin. Gob munched spoonful after spoonful of his breakfast, slurped the milk, and ate the spoon. He devoured the bowl and the cereal box. Everything sloshed around in his plump tummy, including the bowling ball and the cowboy hat he'd eaten earlier in the morning. He let out an enormous burp.

At other tables, monsters dug into their midnight meals—raw steaks and rotten apples, Jell-O and snow cones.

The school bell was ringing! Monsters of all kinds were hurrying through the forest to get to class on time. Bonesy had an enormous backpack hung around his shoulder blade. He caught up to Woolee. Ahead of them loomed the turrets and towers of Monster High. The moon was full. Fog hung low.

Draculaura knew that this must all seem very strange to the Normies. But to her—and a bunch of swamp things, werewolves, vampires, and mummies coming together—it was just Monday.

But how it came to be normal for Draculaura, and how she and her friend Frankie Stein brought monsters from all over the world together, is a kind of amazing story. And it all began one night not so very long ago...